E   **Child Coll**   c.1
FAR

Farber, Norma

  A ship in a storm on the way to
Tarshish.

CHILDREN'S LITERATURE COLLECTION

FREDERICK NOBLE SCHOOL LIBRARY

Gift of Francelia Butler

A SHIP IN A STORM
ON THE WAY TO TARSHISH

by Norma Farber • pictures by Victoria Chess

Greenwillow Books
A Division of William Morrow & Company, Inc.
New York

E
FAR
c. 1

Library of Congress Cataloging
in Publication Data   4/79

Farber, Norma.
A ship in a storm
on the way to Tarshish.
Summary: An up-to-date version of
Jonah and the whale told in verse.
[1.   Whales—Fiction.   2.   Stories
in rhyme]   I.   Chess, Victoria.   II.
Title.   PZ8.3.F224Sh   [E]
77-23288   ISBN 0-688-80096-3
ISBN 0-688-84096-5 lib. bdg.

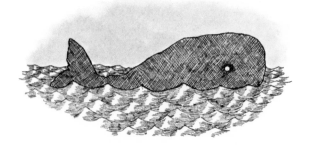

for Ellen, keen sailor

A ship in a storm on the way to Tarshish,
terrible storm at sea!
Waves are crashing,
lines are lashing,
masts are smashing,
sails are ripping,
sailors are tripping,
the hull is shuddering like a leaf.
I think the bow has struck a reef!

Midships, another!
Another! Another!

Time to lower a raft, I think.
Any minute our ship will sink
in a storm on the way to Tarshish.

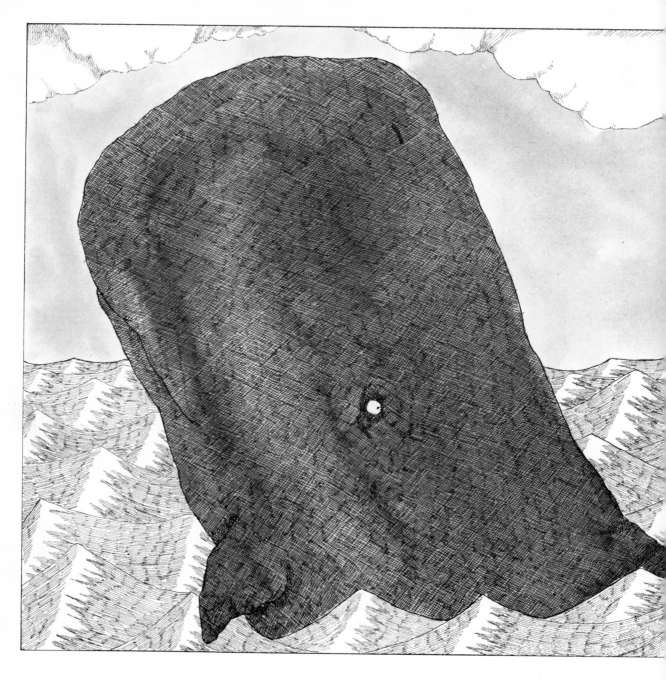

But that's no reef up under the bow!
It's moving, moving amidships now!
Look at it leap!
Look at it dive!
Deep!

It's alive!
It's bumping aft!
Don't lower the raft!
Look at that tail!
By Jehovah, a whale!

He's rolling his eyes
and clapping his jaws.
Brace for a blow.
He's nudging the hull as though, as though
the ship were his *mother!*

Look through the glass,
to find, if we can, the pod he belongs to,
the family he's calling his lonely songs to.
If only,
if only we knew which way they swam
in a storm on the way to Tarshish . . .

Nothing? No rubbery mountains?
No churning mass
of flukes upsetting the tide?
No fountains
of spumy brine?
Nothing? Not a sign?

Wham! Bam! Scram!
He'll stave us to splints if he doesn't stop . . .
There he blows!
Hang on! He's heaving the poop!
Oh quick, before the ship capsizes,
somebody help him find his group!
Who, me?
I see . . .

I'm putting my wet-suit on for the ride.

Easy does it.

I'll sit on your deck.

You'd rather I'd slide right in?

You win.

Down the hatch!

This cabin's great!
I'll put up a periscope, and watch.
The sun is setting golden red.
The wind's subsiding.

Oooh! Look at that wreck!
That squid, how odd!
Those shoals of herring and cod!

Those weeds!
Full steam ahead
in a whale on the way to Tarshish.

Spring of the year:
a sensible whale
plows north. Look there,
Polaris has just ignited his flare!
That heavenly starfish lights our way.

We'll steer by him.
Who needs
a compass? (Will you lower your tail?
I'm trying to keep my ship in view.)

Oh don't give up! There's hope
in a periscope.
Look up where a star is true
till the break of day.
Just let me know
when you want to blow.
We can't go wrong.
And sing, keep singing, I like that song.

And listen!
Catching a tune?
Soon, soon.
Your mother is bound to be calling to you.
Keep north and north in a sea beeline.

Danger! Swim off! A swordfish sword!
What sport to be riding submarine
in a whale on the way to Tarshish!

What's this?
A lump of ambergris!
Hooray, a clue!
Just stay on course, we can't be far.
I'm keeping my eye on a northern star.
Sing, sing loud, as sounds slip by:
shrimp-click, seal-whistle, beluga-squeak,
octopus-hiss and porpoise-shriek.

Reverse! Reverse!
Great white sharks—there's nothing worse!
Dive way down till we're scraping earth.
Give those killers a deep, wide berth.

Now up and on!
The star's a diamond eye,
till dawn slips in with a stronger light.
Sail on! (Your song has swum the night.)
Oh hear the answering family chorus
welcome you back to the fold.

Ahoy! Ahoy!
A fire-black glow,
leviathans all, they rise before us.
Small and young.
Great and old.
The happy reunion of whales is sung.

Steady now! Steady! *Hold* it! Whew!
Stop whirling
and furling,
curving
and swerving,

zooming,

carooming,

jumping

and thumping!

Wait! Don't rock! Don't roll me about!
Don't nuzzle your mother yet!

Safe in her flippers
at last—Hey, wait! Just let
a fellow disembark.

Sun's up, so ease me out.
I think I'll stay on land awhile.

See you sometime again.
Send me a whale-song now and then.
Name's Jonah. Joe, for short.

Never did get to Tarshish
over a stormy sea.
Will I ever get over the whale
that happened to me?
Lucky I'm here to tell the tale.
So's he!